Bilal's Brilliant Bee

MICHAEL ROSEN

ILLUSTRATED BY TONY ROSS

Andersen Press
London

First published in 2016 by
Andersen Press Limited
20 Vauxhall Bridge Road
London SW1V 2SA

www.andersenpress.co.uk

2 4 6 8 10 9 7 5 3 1

British Library Cataloguing in Publication Data available.

ISBN 978 1 78344 395 6

Printed and bound in Great Britain
by Clays Limited, Bungay, Suffolk, NR35 1ED.

Chapter One

Bilal was in terrible trouble. It was the Test.

NOT THE TEST?
YES, THE TEST.
Not just any old test.
It was the special headteacher's test.
This is how the headteacher's test worked . . .

On Monday, Bilal's teacher, Ms Hopeful, told the class a whole load of stuff to do with Henry VIII.

On Tuesday, Ms Hopeful told the class a whole load of stuff to do with spellings.

On Wednesday, Ms Hopeful told the class a whole load of stuff to do with times tables.

On Thursday, Ms Hopeful told the class a whole load of stuff to do with bones.

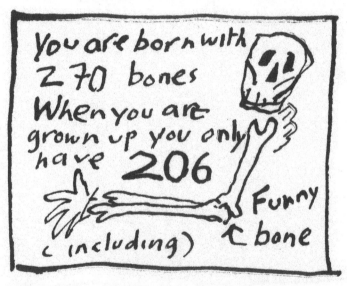

On Friday, the headteacher, Mrs Frown, came into Bilal's class and asked them all a load of questions about Henry VIII, spellings, times tables and bones.

This was the Test.

Now it was the middle of the Test.

Bilal realised that he didn't know any of the answers.

Somehow, for some reason or another, nothing that Ms Hopeful had said to the class had stuck in his mind.

NOTHING AT ALL?

NOPE, NOTHING AT ALL.

He thought he was the only one who didn't know the answers.

So Bilal was feeling awful.

Bilal was feeling desperate.

Bilal was feeling very, very, very, very sad.

Chapter Two

That night Bilal talked to his grandmother, Nanu, about it.

He said, "In the Test, Mrs Frown gave us the question, 'What did Henry VIII have for breakfast?'"

"Are you sure?" said Nanu.

"Hmmm, no, I'm not sure," he said, "but I'm sure I couldn't answer the question."

"Maybe that's you inventing things again," his nanu said.

"The next question said, 'Can you spell the really hard word which was eighteenth on your list of spellings?'"

"Did they really ask you that?" said Nanu.

"Hmmm, I'm not sure," Bilal said, "but I'm sure I couldn't answer the question. Then, the next question said, 'Write out the thirteen-and-a-half times table.'"

"Your thirteen-and-a-half times table?" said Nanu.

"Hmmm, no, I'm not sure," he said.

"These questions are like the things you've invented, Bilal," said Nanu.

"Then there was a question about bones, and the question was, 'Who was Billy Bones?'" Bilal said.

Nanu said, "*That* was the question about bones?"

"Hmmm, I'm not sure," said Bilal. "Sometimes the paper I'm reading goes squiggly and wiggly and figgly."

Nanu said, "You mustn't worry, Bilal. Your trouble is you worry and then it's the worries that stop you doing the answers. You're a good boy and you're wonderful at thinking and inventing things. I remember that time you went to a fancy-dress party with two bits of bread stuck over your ears. When they asked you what you were, you said you were a sandwich!"

Later, Bilal was in bed, and he was worrying about what would happen to him on Monday morning when everyone would hear how they got on in the Test. He would come bottom of the class. Everyone else would laugh at him for knowing absolutely nothing and being absolutely no good at remembering things.

Just as Bilal was thinking all these thoughts, he heard a buzzing sound. Then, the buzzing stopped and he heard someone say in a buzzy sort of voice:

"You mustn't worry, Bilal. Your trouble is you worry."

"Who said that?" said Bilal.

 said the voice.

"Who are you?" said Bilal.

"I've got a bee? I didn't know I had a bee," said Bilal.

"You do now," said the bee, "and something else: I can do whatever you want."

"That's great," said Bilal. "Right. There is something I want straight away. I need to know what's going to happen to me on Monday morning when I hear about the Test."

"Ah, no, hang on," said the bee. "I meant to tell you, I don't do the future. I don't know anything to do with what's going to happen next."

"Oh," said Bilal, "you're not as good as you said you were, then."

"No," said the bee, "it's one of the bad things about me. I tell people that I can do stuff even when I can't."

"OK," said Bilal, "what CAN you do?"

"I am very, very, very good at answering questions," said the bee. "I don't think I can help you with that inventing you do, but so long as it's questions, I can do it."

Bilal thought about that. How could someone be no good at inventing, but be really good at answering questions? Hmmm, interesting problem, he thought, and Bilal liked problems . . .

But no time for that now, he thought. *I've got my own bee! Perhaps . . . maybe . . . he might be able to help me answer questions in tests.*

"Er, do you think you could help me answer the questions we get in the Test?"

"Yep! That's my sort of thing. Oh! I haven't told you who I am."

"Who are you?"

"I'm Bumble. It's my name. Bumble Bee. I didn't come up with that. It was my mum, I think."

"Right, er, Bumble," said Bilal, "the Test. If you're helping me, won't everyone see you buzzing about?"

"Good point. A very good point. How about if I hide somewhere?"

"Yes!" said Bilal. "What about in my pencil case?"

"Your pencil case? Is it smelly?"

"I don't know," said Bilal. "I've never been in there. How about you give it a try?"

So Bumble climbed into Bilal's pencil case.

"How are you doing?" said Bilal.

"It's very dark in here . . ." said Bumble.

"I can open the zip, if you like."

"And it smells."

"I can't do anything about that," said Bilal. "What's it smell of?"

"Er . . . onion," said Bumble.

"Oh – sorry, I hid an onion bhaji in there the other day."

"That's OK," said Bumble. "I like onion bhajis."

Now all seemed set for next week's test.

Chapter Three

It was the Test again. Bilal hadn't done very well last time. In fact, he had done very badly. And the other children *had* laughed at him.

But this time, things were going to be different.

This week Mrs Frown was asking questions about:

The Romans
Rhyming words
Subtraction
and
Water.

Once again, none of it was making any sense.

But just as Bilal started getting worried and the page started going squiggly and wiggly and figgly, he heard a little buzz coming from his pencil case.

Of course, now was the time to see if Bumble could help.

He eased open the zip on the pencil case a couple of centimetres more and Bumble buzzed to say he liked the fresh air.

Mrs Frown was on to it straight away.

"Bilal," she called out, "what are you doing?"

"I'm just getting a pencil," said Bilal.

"What was that buzzing sound?" Mrs Frown asked.

"That was . . . er . . . me . . . I've got something in my throat," Bilal said, doing some quick inventing.

"Do you usually buzz when you're clearing your throat, Bilal?"

The other children laughed.

"I find it helps, if, if, I've . . . er . . . got something like a bit of onion stuck in there," Bilal invented.

"Good one," whispered Bumble from inside the case, making sure not to buzz this time.

Then came the questions:

Question 1
What did Roman soldiers wear under their little leather skirts?

Bumble whispered, "Little leather pants."

So Bilal wrote down, "Little leather pants."

Question 2
What rhymes with 'nothing'?

Bumble whispered, "Nothing rhymes with 'nothing'."

So Bilal wrote down, "Nothing rhymes with 'nothing'."

Question 3
A man has got 103 pies.
He eats 87 pies.
What has he got now?

"A bellyache," whispered Bumble.
Bilal wrote down, "A bellyache."

Question 4
If you freeze orange juice, you get iced orange juice. If you freeze water, you get iced water. What do you get if you freeze ink?

"Iced ink," said Bumble.

"Ugh, you stink!" said Bilal.

"That's because I'm in your pencil case," said the bee.

And Bilal wrote, "Iced ink."

When Mrs Frown marked his test, she stopped frowning. All the answers Bumble gave were right. Well, OK, not the one about the 103 pies. But Mrs Frown said that because Bilal had made her laugh, she didn't mind. Just this once. So Bilal did brilliantly! And the other children didn't laugh at him at all. They laughed at the bellyache joke, but that wasn't laughing AT him.

Chapter Four

When Bilal's nanu came to meet him from school, he rushed up to her and told her that everything was OK in the Test because his bee had helped him.

Nanu looked at Bilal for a moment and said, "That's good. Everyone needs a good friend."

Lovely boy, she thought, *he invents such funny things.*

Later, they were watching TV.

It was the world-famous quiz show, **WHAT'S WHAT? WIN THE LOT!**

Each week, the questionmaster Jack What asked the contestant 101 questions. If the contestant could answer them all in time, they would win all the prizes in the studio. So far, no one in the history of the show had ever answered all 101 questions. So no one had ever won all the prizes in the studio.

Up came the first question: "What colour is an orange?"

"Orange," whispered Bumble from inside Bilal's pencil case.

"Orange!" shouted Bilal.

"Very good," said his nanu. "Did your bee tell you that?" she asked, smiling.

"Yep," said Bilal proudly.

"I think I knew that one too," said Nanu, "but the first ones are always fairly easy."

The second question was: "Does the Earth go round the Sun, or does the Sun go round the Earth?"

"The Earth goes round the Sun," whispered Bumble.

"The Earth goes round the Sun," said Bilal.

"Did you learn that in school?" said Nanu.

"Nope," said Bilal, "that was the bee again."

"Lovely," said Nanu, smiling, thinking about how nice it was to have such an inventive grandson.

. . . And on and on it went . . . till the questions were getting really, really hard.

"Question number eighty-four. What does DNA stand for?"

"Deoxyribonucleic acid," whispered Bumble.

"Deoxyribonucleic acid," said Bilal.

"I don't know," said the contestant on the TV.

Nanu jumped up. "Bilal knows," she shouted.

"He can't hear you," said Bilal.

"I can," whispered Bumble. "I'm doing good, eh?"

"You know what this means, Bilal?" said Nanu. "You HAVE to go on **WHAT'S WHAT? WIN THE LOT!** You'll be the first ever ever ever to win the lot. This is so exciting!"

Chapter Five

A month later and Bilal and his nanu were at the MegaBigMega TV Studios, waiting to step up and sit in the **WHAT'S WHAT? WIN THE LOT!** chair.

Bilal was looking at all the prizes in the studio which he hoped in a few minutes' time would be all his. There were bags and bags of gold coins and loads of digital stuff – TVs, computers, tablets. And best of all, people would cheer him and be impressed, rather than laughing at him and thinking he knew nothing.

"And our next contestant," said Jack What, "is Bilal!"

There was deafening applause.

Bilal stepped forwards and sat in the chair behind the **WHAT'S WHAT? WIN THE LOT!** table.

"Hi Bilal," said Jack What.

"Hi," said Bilal.

"Are you ready to play, **WHAT'S WHAT? WIN THE LOT!**?"

"Yep," said Bilal.

More deafening applause.

"What's your lucky mascot?" said Jack What.

"My lucky mascot is my pencil case," said Bilal.

"Great!" said Jack What. "I bet you've got something in there that could *sharpen* you up, eh?"

For a moment, Bilal thought Jack What knew that Bumble was in there, but then he worked out that Jack What was making some kind of joke about pencil sharpeners.

Bilal tried to laugh at Jack What's joke, but it came out a bit like a cough.

Never mind.

It was time to get on with the quiz.

Once again, the questions started off pretty easy.

"Tell me one thing you might find in a chocolate biscuit?" said Jack What.

whispered Bumble.

said Bilal.

"Correct," said Jack What.

"You love chocolate, don't you?" said Jack What.

Bilal nodded.

Deafening applause.

"Well done, Bilal," said Nanu, but she was way over on the other side of the studio, so Bilal couldn't hear her.

Around about question 34, the questions started getting harder.

"What is rust?" said Jack What.

 whispered Bumble.

 said Bilal.

"Correct!" said Jack What.

Deafening applause.

"Oh, well done, well done, well done, Bilal," said Nanu.

"Could you please sit down?" said the man behind her.

Nanu looked at him. *Hmm, he looks a bit like a tiger*, she thought. *I had better do what he says.*

Around question number 93, the studio was getting seriously excited. Jack What could hardly say the questions.

"What is the French word for a bumblebee?"

"Easy," whispered Bumble, "*un bourdon.*"

"*Un bourdon,*" said Bilal.

Questions 94, 95, 96, 97, 98 and 99 were even harder.

And then it was time for question 100.

This one would be so hard that no one could possibly know this one.

"Question one hundred," said Jack What. "Who won the FA Cup in 1894?"

Surely Bilal wouldn't know that one. The audience held their breath. Nanu closed her eyes.

There was a pause.

Oh no – it looked like Bumble didn't know this one.

The big clock was ticking.

No whisper was coming from the pencil case.

Then . . .

"Sorry," whispered Bumble, "I was just giving my wings a wiggle. The answer is Notts County."

"Notts County," said Bilal.

"Correct!!!" said Jack What. "Everybody, please, get ready for the last and final question: question number one hundred and one."

The audience went crazy.

Nanu was now just rocking to and fro
. . . until the man behind her tapped her
on the shoulder and said, "Excuse me,
could you please stop rocking?"

Nanu remembered his tigerish face
and stopped immediately.

"Audience in the studio," said Jack
What. "I'm going to ask you to be quiet

as we approach this historic moment, when we might, just possibly might, have the world's first ever winner of **WHAT'S WHAT? WIN THE LOT!**"

People all over the world were calling people to their TV sets to come and see Bilal get all these answers right. By now four billion people were watching **WHAT'S WHAT? WIN THE LOT!**

Jack What looked into the camera and said, "Don't go away, see you after the break."

Another billion people who had just been texted by their friends to get to a TV set or computer nearby had switched on or gathered round.

In cities all over the world, cafes with TV sets were filling up with people.

Mountaineers stopped climbing their mountains, switched on their extra-special mountaineering tablets, and got a signal to watch.

Lonely shepherds, miles from anywhere, were being told what was happening on their mobiles. Their sheep stood still, waiting for a sign from the shepherds to tell them how Bilal was doing.

People in hospitals were demanding that their beds be shunted nearer to the TV so that they could get a look.

Chapter Six

"And now something I've never said before on **WHAT'S WHAT? WIN THE LOT!**" said Jack What.

As everyone all over the world took in a breath all at the same time, it made the whole Earth do a little shake. TV sets shook on top of tables. This made some TV sets turn off and people rushed over and kicked them back into life.

What would question number 101 be?
They didn't have to wait long.

"What is the number on the barcode
on the label on the bottle of water in
my pocket?"

All over the world people said,

Barcode!

On the label on his bottle of water?

That's not fair!

How can he know that one?

It's just to cheat him from winning the lot

Nanu was crying with rage that it was so unfair.

The man behind tapped her on the shoulder and said, "I'm sorry to ask you again, but could you please stop doing that?"

Nanu stopped crying. She didn't want to be eaten by a tiger.

Bilal was waiting for Bumble. He was starting to get nervous.

There was silence.

Bumble whispered, "Sorry, but I just don't know. It's just something I can't answer. I'm really sorry, but you'll have to make something up. It'll be all right, Bilal."

Bilal thought for a moment. He didn't have long. Jack What was raising his Time Out Wand which he used to bring the game to a stop.

What could Bilal do? Oh no, was he going to lose **WHAT'S WHAT? WIN THE LOT!** at the very last moment?

Well, this is what happened:

Bilal invented something. All by himself. He used his imagination and thought, *Maybe . . . maybe there is no bottle of water? Maybe it's a trick question. Yes . . . a trick question!!!!*

So Bilal said, "The barcode says nothing. Because there is no barcode. There is no bottle of water in your pocket."

There was another pause.

Jack What leaned forward.

Had Bilal got it right? Or had he got it wrong?

All over the world, people took in another breath. The Earth took another shudder and a glass jug fell to the floor in a cafe in Nairobi and made everyone jump.

"CORRECT!" said Jack What. "WHAT'S WHAT? YOU'VE WON THE LOT!!!"

And the world went crazy.

There was dancing in the streets,
flags were waved at the North Pole,

bands began to play where people hadn't heard a band in the previous 46 years, babies who had just been born decided that they wouldn't cry and laughed instead.

The audience in the studio were standing up, and some people clapped so hard their hands fell off.

Nanu wasn't daring to do very much in case the tiger behind her jumped on her back.

But Bilal was worrying a bit. Perhaps he shouldn't have gone in for the quiz with Bumble helping him? Wasn't it cheating?

"Now one last thing," said Jack What. "As you know, ladies and gentlemen, before we give out all the prizes in the studio, we have to do our little check that you, Bilal, used no special help, no electronic device, no extra help from an external source. Step forward for the check."

Bilal stood up and everyone watched.

"Don't forget to pick up your mascot, your pencil case, Bilal," said Jack What. "It's just like the security machines at the airport."

Then in walked two Security Checkers, wheeling the radio-sensitive, gamma-ray-receiving chamber.

Bilal was asked to walk into the Security Chamber.

There was quiet while the world waited.

QUIET.

MORE QUIET.

YET MORE QUIET.

Would the radio-sensitive, gamma-ray-receiving chamber spot Bumble inside the pencil case???

Suddenly:

DZAZZINGGG!!!

The Security Checkers' radio-sensitive, gamma-ray-receiving chamber's alarm went off.

The cheering and applause came to a sudden standstill.

Everyone looked at Bilal.

What had the boy got on him? Had he put some kind of secret wire in his ear?

WAS BILAL THE AMAZING QUIZ CONTESTANT A . . .

. . .CHEAT???!!!!

Chapter Seven

In the hospital lab, 39 TOP-LEVEL scientists were investigating Bilal.

They had already run 185 tests on him, and were now working on another 74.

Nanu was at his side.

"You mustn't worry, Bilal," she said. "Worrying stops you doing the things you're good at, like thinking and inventing."

Outside, thousands of people from TV stations and newspapers were telling and writing their stories for the news:

Inside the hospital lab, Bumble was talking to Bilal.

"Just tell them," he said. "Tell 'em I helped you with the questions up to one hundred."

"I can't," said Bilal. "If I tell them, people will know that I am the world's biggest cheat. I will be in every newspaper and on every TV station in the world, no one will ever talk to me ever again and Mrs Frown will say that I have let the school down, and worst of all, Nanu will be totally so disappointed with me."

"You answered the last question by yourself," pointed out Bumble. "The hardest one of all."

"I'm still afraid that everyone will be very cross," said Bilal.

"Just tell them," said the bee. "You have to be honest. It'll work out, believe me."

On went the tests.

After three weeks, they found ...

... nothing.

"Nothing!" screamed the TV reporters.

Bilal was taken out of the hospital, driven back to the studio in MegaBigMega TV Studio's limo.

Jack What was there, waiting for him.

"Ladies and gentlemen, followers of **WHAT'S WHAT? WIN THE LOT!** will know by now that the world's first winner of **WHAT'S WHAT? WIN THE LOT!** has passed all the tests."

"Bilal, I am pleased to say that MegaBigMega TV Studios will in just one moment, present you with all the prizes in the studio . . . but before we do, can I ask you one last question?"

"You know and I know that when you stepped into our special Security Chamber, you set off the alarm. Yet when we ran the tests on you, we found nothing. As you have shown us, you know the answers to any question we throw at you. So why, why oh why, do you think the alarm went off?"

Bumble whispered:

"Because," said Bilal, "I have a bee and it tells me everything. Well, nearly everything."

There was a moment of complete hush . . .

. . . apart from Nanu, who was giggling.

She turned to the woman next to her and said, "Oh, that's Bilal again. Him and his inventing! Always on about his bee!"

But Bilal was thinking something very different.

And then Jack What laughed.

Then the studio audience laughed, the people clustered round their TV sets, mobiles, computers and tablets laughed, and soon the whole world was laughing so hard that the world did a judder and a small volcano on an island in the South Pacific erupted, luckily causing no casualties because everyone had left the island to watch Bilal on the TV.

"Very good," said Jack What. "Not only a wonderful quiz contestant, but a great comedian too! Bilal, the prizes are all yours."

"All because of his inventing," said Nanu.

Chapter Eight

Outside the studio, in a small office, Bilal and his nanu had to sign a little bit of paper.

Back home, Bilal and Nanu started to unwrap the prizes.

I'm afraid to say, things weren't as they hoped.

The TV sets and digital gear didn't work.

PAH!!!

What looked like bags of gold, turned out to be bags of chocolate wrapped in gold paper.

"Nanu," said Bilal, "we have to tell all the TV companies and newspapers about this."

"Er . . ." said Nanu.

"What?" said Bilal.

"Do you remember that little bit of paper we signed?"

"Yes," said Bilal.

"Well, it said that we mustn't tell anyone anything about the prizes. And we signed that."

"Oh no!!!" said Bilal.

"Oh yes!!!" said Nanu. "Never mind, let's just eat the chocolate."

In bed, Bumble said, "See, Bilal, I told you it would work out."

"What are you talking about?" said Bilal. "All I got was a few bags of chocolate money."

"Oh?! I thought you liked chocolate," said Bumble. "And you did miss some time off school, didn't you? That's been fun, eh?"

"Yes, I do like chocolate," said Bilal, "but I thought I'd won millions of pounds of stuff."

"True. But best of all," said Bumble, "you managed to answer a question all by yourself. Without my help. And not any old question, but the hardest one of all: the last question in **WHAT'S WHAT? WIN THE LOT!**"

Bilal lay in bed, his eyes wide open, glistening with the thought of it. "That's true . . . I've never got a question right by myself before!"

"And all because you are good at inventing things!" said the bee. "You know, Bilal, maybe you aren't perfect at knowing answers to questions when you're asked, just like I'm not very good at saying what's going to happen next. But you ARE great at coming up with ideas, imagining things."

"I suppose I am . . ." said Bilal.

"And although you'll probably have to do the Test at school again, at least now everyone is so proud of you for winning **WHAT'S WHAT? WIN THE LOT!**, they won't laugh at you. They know you can answer the hardest questions of all – the ones you need to invent answers to."

"Maybe you can help me with the Test again."

"Maybe . . ." said the bee.

Just then there was a sudden gust of wind and the window blew open. As it blew open, the wind rushed in and then as it swirled about, the wind rushed out again.

Nothing strange about that.

Other than . . . other than . . . other than . . . when the wind rushed out it took Bumble with it.

BUMBLE WHOOSHED OUT OF THE WINDOW.

"Bumble!" Bilal shouted.

"What's that? What's going on, Bilal?"
Nanu said, running into the room.

"My bee, Bumble, my bee, he's gone
. . . he's flown out the window."

Nanu looked at her beloved Bilal. *Such a funny boy. Such a clever, funny boy, making up all these things about a bee . . .*

She ruffled his hair and tucked him back into bed.

Bilal lay in bed, looking up at the ceiling.

At first, all he could think of was the Test and all the questions he couldn't answer.

How awful was that?!

But then, the more he thought about it, he started to see that maybe it was a good thing that Bumble had been blown out of the window.

After all, if he kept on answering questions with Bumble's help, maybe one day he would be found out. Answering questions wasn't much fun anyway, and the prizes weren't as special as everyone said they would be. No, the best bit was inventing things and imagining things.

Now, he said to himself, *I want to get better and better at that.*

So it was all OK, all good . . . he thought of Bumble, his very own bee who had helped him so much, and as he thought of that, a smile came to his face.

I wonder where he is now, he thought,
I wonder . . .

. . . and he dozed off still wondering.

Hmmmm.

Yes, WHERE IS BUMBLE NOW?????

Well, let's just say he goes wherever people are being asked lots and lots and lots of questions, and he helps people who need help remembering things. So look around – he might be in your classroom now!